JENNY OLDFIELD

Storm Cloud

With illustrations by
Gary Blythe

Barrington Stoke

A huge thank you to the staff of
Lost Valley Ranch, Colorado, for their help and
friendship through all the years.

First published in 2017 in Great Britain by
Barrington Stoke Ltd
18 Walker Street, Edinburgh, EH3 7LP

www.barringtonstoke.co.uk

Text © 2017 Jenny Oldfield
Illustrations © 2017 Gary Blythe

The moral right of Jenny Oldfield and Gary Blythe to be identified
as the author and illustrator of this work has been asserted in
accordance with the Copyright, Designs and Patents Act, 1988

A CIP catalogue record for this book is available
from the British Library upon request

ISBN: 978-1-78112-689-9

Printed in China by Leo

Contents

Chapter 1
A Dream Come True

Kami Miller gave her dad a big hug before he left.

"So this is goodbye," he said. "Have a great time at Wolf Ridge Ranch."

"Thanks, Dad," Kami said. "I will."

It was a dream come true to stay at the ranch. Kami would spend the whole summer here with her best friend, Macy Lucas. She'd be working with the horses as a real cowgirl.

Her dad took a step back. "OK – I gotta go," he said. He smiled at Kami and Macy. "Stay safe, both of you."

"We will," they promised.

They watched him get into his car and drive out of the yard up the steep mountain track.

"Are you feeling OK?" Macy asked.

Kami brushed a tear from her eye as the car disappeared round a bend. "Yeah, I'm cool, thanks."

'Bye, Dad,' she thought. 'See you in a few weeks.'

Macy smiled and nodded. "So let's go to the meadow and meet your horse."

N

Kami followed Macy past a big barn into a green meadow. Two horses raised their heads and looked at them.

"The grey one is called Pepper," Macy said. "He's my horse. The brown one is Lady Alice."

Kami watched as Lady Alice took a few steps towards her. Her coat shone in the sun. Her mane and tail were black and silky. "She's beautiful," Kami murmured.

"I'm glad you like her," Macy said. "She's yours for the summer."

Lady Alice kept on coming over the long grass. Beyond the meadow Kami saw snow-capped mountains set against a clear blue sky. A stream ran along the valley bottom and Kami saw three more horses drinking there.

"Hey," she said when Lady Alice came right up to her.

The horse nudged Kami's hand with her soft nose.

Macy laughed. "She says hi."

"Hi." Kami stroked Lady Alice's neck. She longed to jump on her back and ride her up the nearest mountain, past the tall pine trees, higher and higher towards the snow line.

"I reckon you two will get along just fine," Macy said. "Now let's go back to the house and meet the rest of my family."

"So, Kami, you're here to help us fetch cows down from the mountains," Macy's father, Jeff, said.

He was watching the sun go down in a wheelchair on the porch at the front of the house. His hair was grey and his face was thin.

"Sure," Kami said. "But I'll need Macy to show me how."

"We have three hundred head of cattle out there," Jeff told her. "Macy's brother, Wes, is in charge here since I had my fall. He knows where to find cows."

"Hey, so do I," Macy reminded him. "I've been a cowgirl all my life!"

Ella, Macy's mother, came out of the house with a tray of drinks. She was tall and fair like Macy and she was dressed in jeans, a denim shirt and fancy cowboy boots. "How much horse riding have you done?" she asked Kami, as she handed her an iced tea.

"Plenty," Kami replied. "But it's been mostly in an arena up till now."

Ella smiled. "Don't worry, you won't get lost here. There are trails to follow and Lady Alice always knows which way is home."

"Just stick with me, kid," Macy said in a funny voice. "That way you can't go wrong."

Kami loved how her friend never stopped smiling and kidding around. "OK, I will," she said.

Later that night, Kami sat at her bedroom window. The moon was full and bright. Out in the meadow she spotted Macy's grey horse, Pepper, but at first she couldn't pick out Lady Alice from the group. There was a cute black and white mare and a pretty palomino, plus a big, strong sorrel standing close to the gate.

"Hey, Lady Alice, where are you?" Kami murmured.

Then she spotted her horse over by the far fence. Lady Alice stood with a young colt. It was hard to tell in this light, but the colt seemed to be dark brown with a black mane and tail – a skinny, restless youngster with long legs who swished his tail and tossed his head.

'I wonder who that is,' Kami thought.

Then the colt broke away from Lady Alice and set off at a gallop across the star-lit meadow. He bucked as he ran and kicked out with his back legs.

'Wow!' Kami thought. 'That guy's young and full of energy. I'd really like to find out who he is.'

She stayed at the window for a long time, watching the horses. She thought about her dad and mum back home in the city. The house would be empty without her. They would miss her, she knew. But they'd said yes to Macy's invite.

"Go to Wolf Ridge Ranch for the summer and be a cowgirl," they'd insisted. "Don't think about us for even a minute – just go!"

And so here Kami was, gazing out at the moon and stars, longing to ride Lady Alice out into the mountains. "Tomorrow," she said out loud.

As if she'd heard Kami speak, Lady Alice turned her head to look at the house and gazed at Kami.

Kami yawned, stretched then crept back to bed.

"First I have to get some sleep," she told herself.

Chapter 2
Round-up

Next morning Kami got out of bed before it was light. She put on jeans and a T-shirt then tied back her long, dark hair. Then she went downstairs and into the kitchen.

"Hey, Kami. There's eggs and bacon for breakfast," Ella Lucas said. The radio was playing a lively country song and Ella was singing along while she stood at the stove.

Kami sat down next to Jeff. "Where's Macy?" she asked.

"She's out in the corral with Pepper and Lady Alice," Jeff said. "She's giving them an extra feed, so they'll be ready for a busy day."

Kami jumped up from her seat. "Maybe I should go and help."

But Ella made her sit down again. "Eat!" she insisted, as she put a vast plate of food down on the table. "A horse can't do a day's work on an empty stomach and neither can you."

Kami ate fast. She'd almost finished when she heard heavy footsteps out on the porch and a man strode into the kitchen. He was a younger version of Jeff, with broad shoulders and long legs. He wore a red shirt, jeans, cowboy boots and he carried a black Stetson hat.

Ella made a space for him at the table. "Sit down and eat," she said. "Kami, this is Macy's brother, Wes. Wes – Kami."

Wes nodded at Kami as he put his hat on a hook by the door and sat down. His face was serious. "I just drove up to Bear Rock," he said.

"Any cows?" Jeff asked.

"Yep. I saw a couple of mommas and babies up on the ridge and three more pairs over by the old mine shaft."

"That's ten for you and Macy to bring in," Jeff said to Kami. Then he sighed and frowned. "If I wasn't in this damn chair I'd ride out there to do it myself."

Wes frowned too. "We know that, Dad. Relax. Don't beat yourself up."

"That's right," Ella agreed. "It'll take time for you to get better. Let us do the work this year."

"OK, OK," Jeff said, but Kami saw that his teeth were gritted. His pushed his plate away. "I don't have any choice, do I?"

⚡

Out in the corral, Macy had almost finished brushing Pepper and Lady Alice. "Hey, lazy-bones," she said to Kami.

"I'm sorry!" Kami said. "You should have woken me."

"I'm kidding!" Macy laughed. "Here – you can brush Lady Alice's mane while I fetch the saddles."

Kami took the brush and ran it through her horse's long mane to take all the tangles out. Lady Alice and Pepper were tied to a rail next to the barn door. They were happy to stand and wait while Kami brushed and Macy fetched saddles from the tack room.

"I just met Wes," Kami told Macy.

"And?"

"He's seen ten cows near a place called Bear Rock."

"Cool. We'll bring them in." Macy lifted the heavy saddle onto Pepper's back. "Don't mind Wes, by the way."

"What do you mean?" Kami asked.

Macy buckled the girth strap tight under Pepper's belly. "He's been in a bad mood of late, that's all. It's not personal, so don't take it that way."

"OK." Kami grunted as she lifted Lady Alice's saddle and settled it in place on her back. "You're right – he didn't smile much."

"Like I say – ignore him," Macy said. She showed Kami how to put on Lady Alice's bridle and soon they were good to go.

"There are ten cows out by Bear Rock, you say?" Macy asked.

Kami nodded as they both stepped up into the saddle. "Why do we have to round them up and bring them back to the ranch?"

"To brand the babies," Macy explained. "We brand them with the letters W and R, to show everyone they belong to Wolf Ridge Ranch. Then we send them back out onto the mountain for the rest of the summer."

"Cool."

Kami was eager to get to work. The sun was up and there were pink clouds in the pure blue sky. They set off at a brisk pace.

"With luck we'll have those ten in the Far Meadow by noon," Macy told Kami. "Let's go, girl, and find us some cows."

↗

The girls rode out along the Jeep road, past the meadow. Wes was there, putting a halter on the big sorrel horse that Kami had seen in the moonlight.

"That's my brother's horse, Sundance," Macy said. "He's by far the best horse for rounding up cows. He and Wes make a great team."

Kami could picture the pair of them out there in the mountains – both Wes and Sundance were strong and confident. They acted as if nothing could stop them.

As Wes walked Sundance back to the ranch, Kami and Macy rode on until they came to the far end of the meadow.

"The black and white pony by the fence is Mum's horse, Candy," Macy told Kami. "And the palomino down by the creek is called Honey. She was the horse Dad rode before his ... fall." For once the bright smile vanished from her face.

"What happened exactly?" Kami asked.

"Oh, let's not talk about it," Macy said, quick as a whip.

Kami was still full of questions. "Who's that little guy drinking from the creek?" she asked. She'd spotted the playful colt that she'd seen the night before. In the daylight he was even more beautiful. His coat was dark, velvety brown and his mane and tail were pure black.

"We call him Storm Cloud." Macy turned Pepper off the Jeep road up a narrow trail towards some pine trees. "You see that big rock up ahead? That's Bear Rock."

"OK," Kami said. "I'll start looking for cows."

Kami's heart beat faster as she and Lady Alice followed Macy and Pepper up the steep, rugged slope. She spotted a dark shape half hidden behind a rock, but it turned out to be the trunk of a fallen tree. Then something moved behind a bush and her heart raced again. This time it was a little deer that leaped out in front of them as they drew near. The deer jumped the bush then ran up the mountain, out of sight.

"This is harder than I thought," Kami said to Macy. "Those cows could be anywhere by now."

Macy laughed at her. "Yep, city girl – cows
do have legs. They can walk wherever they
like. But look – here's cow poop on the ground.
It's fresh."

Yuck! Kami pulled a face. "But I guess that
means they were just here."

"And here are hoof prints."

Macy was the expert cowgirl now – she
picked up the trail in the soft, dusty ground and
followed it past Bear Rock onto a nearby ridge.

They rode clear of the trees and came
out to a perfect view of the next valley. They
peered around and it was Kami who was first to
spot the black and white cows.

"There's a whole bunch of them!" she cried,
pleased with herself. "Over there, by that big
rock."

The girls rode fast down the hill until they came to the cows. The mommas raised their heads and gazed at them while the babies huddled close to their mothers.

"Take it easy," Macy murmured, to herself as much as to the nervous cows and their calves. She counted ten cows altogether.

Kami pulled on the reins to bring Lady Alice to a stop, and then she sat still and calm in the saddle. She saw the W.R. brand on the mother cows' backsides and a blue tag on their ears with a number on. "What now?" she asked Macy.

"This is perfect," Macy said in a low voice. "We can round up all five pairs in one go and drive them back to the ranch."

Just like that! Kami smiled to herself. Macy made it sound so easy.

But just then the nearest cow made a break from the group. Lady Alice was quick off the mark. Kami sat tight as the horse darted forward to cut off the runaway then drive her back into the group.

"Good job!" Macy said. Then she showed Kami how to get behind the cows and push them towards Bear Rock. "Stay close but not too close. Watch number 33 – she's in the lead. The others will follow her."

The cows raised dust as they walked. They stopped to eat and they pooped as they went along. Walk – eat – poop, up onto the ridge and down again, out of the trees, towards the Jeep road.

Kami copied everything that Macy did. She echoed her cry of "*Yip, cows, yip!*" whenever they slowed down, and she made sure that Lady Alice put pressure on the ones that lagged behind.

The sun rose high in the sky and Kami was glad she was dressed in a cool T-shirt and jeans. 'Cowgirls work hard,' she thought just as a momma cow broke away. Kami and Lady Alice went after her and brought her back into the group.

"Finding it tough?" Macy asked with a grin.

'Yes, but I love it!" Kami said. "We've rounded up ten cows and it's not even midday."

Chapter 3
The Whip

Ten cows in the morning and seven more in the afternoon.

By the end of the day Kami was tired out. She was hot and sweaty and grubby, *and* her butt was sore from riding all day.

But there was still plenty more work to do.

"Good job," Jeff said. He was sitting next to the barn door in his chair. "Walk your horse out to the meadow, Kami. Macy, it looks like Pepper threw a shoe. You need to call the farrier."

"OK, Dad. I'll do it now." Macy turned to Kami. "Can you take Pepper to the meadow for me?"

"Sure."

Kami untied Pepper's lead rope and led him and Lady Alice out of the corral. As she walked them past the barn, she saw Wes lead the young colt out of the meadow. Storm Cloud pulled back and Wes yanked hard on the lead rope to make him move forward. He didn't say "hi" to Kami – he just walked on with a scowl on his face.

Kami reached the meadow then took off the horses' halters. She watched them head for the creek to take a long, cool drink. Then she walked to the Far Meadow to count the cows that had been taken in. She counted 40, which meant that Wes and Sundance had taken in 23 single-handed. It also meant that there were 260 Wolf Ridge cows still roaming free on the mountain.

"That's a lot of cows," Kami said to herself with a low whistle.

The horses were all happy in the meadow, so Kami turned and began the walk back to the ranch house. When she came close to the barn, she heard a shrill neigh followed by a man's voice raised in anger.

Kami's heart missed a beat. What should she do – walk on and ignore it?

The horse neighed again, even shriller this time, and there was a crashing sound. The man yelled and swore.

'No, I can't ignore it,' Kami decided, and she walked around the back of the barn, towards the noise.

What she saw made her heart thud hard against her ribs.

Storm Cloud was inside, in a round pen. Wes stood in the centre of the pen with a long whip. He lashed out at the colt and drove him forward. Storm Cloud's dark coat dripped with sweat. His ears lay flat against his head and his eyes rolled in fear.

Wes raised the whip again and made it snake along the dusty ground. It flicked against Storm Cloud's hooves and drove him crazy with panic. Storm Cloud reared up then crashed down against the high fence. Wes yelled at him in fury and whipped him on.

Kami couldn't believe her eyes. She shook her head as if to shake the horror away, then put her hand to her mouth. She was too shocked to move or say a word.

Poor, poor Storm Cloud!

The horse galloped on, reared again and gave a high whinny. He switched direction to try and escape the whip, but Wes was onto him again, making him run faster, driving him on and on.

"Stop!" Kami shouted at last. "STOP! What are you doing?"

She knew that Wes had heard her, but still he didn't stop. He turned his back on her and used the whip again, snaking it along the ground.

Kami couldn't bear to watch. Her heart pounded as she ran to the house to look for Macy. Jeff was on the front porch, but Macy was nowhere to be seen.

"Kami, what's wrong?" Jeff asked. "You're pale as anything. Is something the matter?"

"Where's Macy?" Kami stammered.

"In the tack room, cleaning bridles."

Kami ignored Jeff's calls as she doubled back and ran into the small, dark tack room. She looked wildly around at the rows of saddles and brackets for bridles and halters. "Macy, where are you?" she yelled. "You've got to come!"

Macy stepped out from behind the door. "Come where?"

"To the round pen behind the barn," Kami said. She was shaking with anger and it was hard to breathe. "Wes is there with Storm Cloud."

"Oh." Macy looked away. Her voice was flat and low.

"Come with me!" Kami said again. "Wes is being really mean. What are you waiting for?"

Macy shook her head. "It's OK. Wes is training Storm Cloud."

"*Training?*" Kami said, like an echo. What she'd seen didn't look like training – it looked like cruelty.

"My brother knows what he's doing," Macy insisted, but she frowned as she brushed past Kami.

Kami followed her out into the corral. "Wes is using a whip and Storm Cloud is scared and hurt!" she said. She was almost shouting now. "It's not right, Macy. You need to come and see."

At last Macy turned to face her. Her eyes were blank. "Listen to me and listen good. Wes has been training colts since he was a little kid. He knows what to do, OK?"

Kami shook her head and groaned. Why was Macy being like this? She felt helpless.

"OK?" Macy said again.

Kami heard the sound of Storm Cloud whinnying. She closed her eyes and shook her head again.

"Wes is the boss around here, in case you didn't know." Macy's voice grew hard. "So butt out, Kami, if you know what's good for you."

And that was it. Macy rammed her hat onto her head and walked off. Kami looked over at the house, where Ella was on the porch with Jeff.

'They must know,' she realised. 'They must all know what Wes does to Storm Cloud back there behind the barn. And there's not a thing I can do.'

⚡

Kami's head was in a total spin. She didn't know what to think. She decided to go for a walk before supper.

"Are you sure you're OK?" Jeff asked her as she set off along the Jeep road.

"I'm sure," she told him. "I just want a breath of air."

She almost ran past the barn and the hidden corral until she came to the first meadow. She stopped there and leaned on the fence to watch the horses. Honey and Candy stood in the creek up to their knees. Sundance and Pepper grazed the long grass while Lady Alice and Storm Cloud stood by the far fence. When they saw Kami they walked over to her.

Kami compared the two horses. They had the same dark manes and tails, but the colt's coat was darker and he had a white stripe down his nose that the older horse didn't have. An idea struck her and she knew it was true.

Storm Cloud was Lady Alice's baby!

That was how come they stayed together in the meadow and didn't join in with the other horses. They were mother and son.

Storm Cloud hung back as if he didn't trust Kami, but Lady Alice came up to the fence. Kami stroked the mare's nose. "Hey," she

whispered. "Do you know what happens to your baby? Do you hear him in the round pen?"

Lady Alice gave a long, loud sigh as if she understood every word.

"I guess you do," Kami murmured, and she put her arms round Lady Alice's neck.

After a while Kami walked on. She stood on the wooden bridge that crossed the creek and looked over the Far Meadow.

'Wolf Ridge Ranch is so beautiful,' she thought. It was miles from anywhere. The mountains rose out of the valley and went on for ever. The sky was the purest blue.

"I'm a guest here and Macy is my best friend," Kami reminded herself. She spoke out loud to get her thoughts in order. "She's lived here all her life. I've only been here a day or two. What makes me think I know better than her?"

She looked down at the clear stream flowing beneath her feet. "If Macy says that Wes knows how to train colts, she must be right," she told herself.

'But she's not,' a little voice said in her head. 'It's not right to use a whip and drive a colt half crazy. It's not right to make him sweat and run him into the ground. What's the point of that?'

So what had been going on when Macy refused to find out what her big brother was up to? That was the real puzzle. Kami remembered Macy's cold, angry voice when she'd told her to butt out. 'That's so not like her,' she realised. 'The Macy I know is friendly and upbeat, not heartless and cruel.'

The water flowed on over smooth pebbles. It lapped at the grassy banks.

"Oh, I get it!" Kami said. She opened her eyes wide and gazed at the far-off, snowy mountains. "Macy is scared of Wes. So are Jeff and Ella. They all are."

And, with that thought ringing in her mind, Kami set off back to the ranch.

Chapter 4
Mother and Son

Kami sat down at the supper table. Macy was beside her and Wes sat opposite. Ella was carving slices of beef while Jeff served the vegetables.

"What's the plan for tomorrow?" Jeff asked Wes, as he loaded his plate with potatoes.

"There are around fifty cows out by Clearwater," Wes replied in a gruff voice. "I want us to ride out there and bring them in."

"I'll come too," Ella said. "You'll need plenty of help."

"Clearwater is a lake to the north of here," Jeff told Kami. "It's a two-hour ride."

"Four hours on the way back," Ella added. "We'll be pushing a bunch of cows, remember."

Kami stopped listening. She would have been excited at the prospect before, but now her head was full of how she could save Storm Cloud from Wes's cruel training routine.

"... Kami?" Macy tapped her on the arm. "I said – can you pass me the potatoes, please?"

In a daze, Kami passed her the bowl. She snuck a look at Wes, who was eating and not talking. He seemed to have a lot on his mind.

'Does he ever smile?' Kami wondered. There were frown lines on his face and his movements were sudden and jerky.

Wes looked up and caught Kami staring at him. His frown deepened as he pushed his plate away. "We need to be ready to leave at 6.30," he said. "That includes you, Kami."

"I'll be there," she promised.

His stern look told her that he didn't think she could do it, but Kami was determined to show him he was wrong.

Wes left the table and grabbed his hat from its hook. "Macy, the farrier's here to put new shoes on Pepper."

Macy jumped up and followed him out. "I'll go fetch Pepper from the meadow. Kami, you get an early night."

"Good idea," Ella agreed.

So Kami finished her supper and went upstairs to get ready for bed. When she looked out of her window she saw a white truck in

the corral and the farrier at work putting new
shoes on Pepper. The man finished and Macy
led Pepper back out to the meadow. The sun
was setting behind the mountains. The sky was
reddish-gold.

'How can I help Storm Cloud?' Kami
wondered over and over.

Half an hour later, she was sitting up in
bed with a book when there was a knock at the
door. It was Macy, still in her jeans and T-shirt.
"Cool – you're not asleep," she said as she
closed the door behind her.

"I was thinking about Storm Cloud," Kami
admitted.

"That's what I want to talk to you about."
Macy sat at the end of the bed. "There's
something I need to tell you."

"Go ahead."

"I'm sorry about what I said earlier about how you should butt out. I was rude."

"That's OK."

"It's a touchy subject and this is why." Macy paused and fiddled with the edge of Kami's bed cover. "Lady Alice is our brood mare. She gave birth to Storm Cloud fifteen months ago."

"I guessed that," Kami said. "They look so alike."

"But he's different from her," Macy said. "Lady Alice is laid back. She never spooks or puts a foot wrong. Storm Cloud's the exact opposite. He's never calm. He's always on edge."

"He's still young," Kami pointed out.

"Yeah," Macy said, "but we always knew he was going to be a handful. Even when he was a baby, he kicked out when anyone went near him. Dad wanted to call him Thunder because of the way he acted, but I thought of Storm Cloud and that's the name that stuck. That's why Wes needs to be strict with him when he works with him in the round pen."

"It was worse than strict," Kami broke in. She remembered the crack of the whip and the look of fear in Storm Cloud's eyes.

Macy put up a hand to stop her. "Listen. I haven't told you the important bit yet. Dad was the one who first took Storm Cloud in hand. Early this spring he started work with him in the round pen, as gentle as you like." She paused to clear her throat. "He got him ready to be saddled and bridled. It took four whole weeks."

"Then what happened?" Kami asked.

Macy sighed and when she spoke again her voice was choked. "Like I said, Dad got him used to the idea of being ridden in the end.

But the first time Dad got on his back, Storm Cloud went crazy. He bucked and kicked like a bronco. Dad's a strong rider and at first he stayed on. But Storm Cloud didn't give in. He went on bucking round and round the pen. In the end he stormed right at the fence and jumped clean over it. Dad fell off and broke his back." She paused, and there were tears in her eyes. "That's how come he's in a wheelchair."

"I didn't know," Kami murmured. She leaned forward and put her hand over Macy's. "I'm so sorry."

"It's OK," Macy sniffed. "The doctors say Dad will learn to walk again but it'll take time."

"Now I see why Wes is raging mad with Storm Cloud," Kami said. "He has to be in charge of the ranch while your dad gets better." Jeff's accident had put him out of action at a time when his family needed him the most.

"Exactly." Macy took a deep breath. "Wes wasn't always this way. He used to be fun, not all scowly and angry."

Kami nodded.

"And he's not really mean. Deep down, he wouldn't harm a fly."

Kami wasn't so sure, but this wasn't the time to argue. The Lucas family had had a hard time and she didn't want to make it worse. But still she couldn't forget what she'd seen in the round pen.

"So we're friends again?" Macy asked as she got ready to leave.

"Friends," Kami agreed. "Always."

"Cool. I'll see you tomorrow. Six o'clock, rise and shine."

"Yes, six o'clock," Kami said with a grin.

Macy left the bedroom. Outside the sky grew dark, but Kami didn't sleep. She was scared that she would dream about a dark bay colt running inside a round pen. She tried to shut out the memory of Storm Cloud with his ears flat against his head, sweating and breathing hard, driven crazy by the whip that snaked around his hooves.

So Kami stayed awake, staring out at the moon and praying for an answer that refused to come.

Chapter 5
Saving Storm Cloud

The next day, just as planned, Kami rode Lady Alice to Clearwater Lake. She worked hard with Macy, Ella and Wes to round up the cows and bring them home safe.

"How do you like being a cowgirl?" Ella asked Kami as at last they drove 52 tired cows into the Far Meadow.

"I love it!" Kami said and it was true. She loved the mountains and the clear blue lake, the *yip-yip* cowgirl yell and the warm glow she felt when at last they closed the gate on the cows in the meadow.

They were tired and hungry as they rode on towards the ranch house. Wes rode Sundance ahead of the others. He unsaddled his horse in the main corral then rushed off alone.

"I'll go and see how your dad is," Ella told Macy. "The horses deserve an extra feed. Can you two girls take them into the feed stalls?"

"Sure thing," Macy and Kami said.

They took off the saddles then led Lady Alice, Pepper and Candy into the stalls down the side of the barn. Kami tied them to the rail while Macy tipped grain into the mangers.

Then Kami heard the sound she'd been dreading. It was Storm Cloud's whinny – high and shrill – and it meant only one thing. Wes had started work with the colt in the round pen. *Oh, God!*

Kami's stomach turned. She couldn't bear to hear that awful sound. Without thinking, she ran towards the pen.

"Kami, come back!" Macy cried. She dropped the bucket of grain and followed.

Kami ran down the centre of the barn and turned the corner. She saw Wes and Storm Cloud and it was worse than before. This time Wes had tied an empty plastic sack to Storm Cloud's tail. The blue sack flapped as the colt galloped, and it was scaring him half to death. But Wes wouldn't let him stop. He drove him on with the whip.

"Oh my God!" Macy murmured as she caught up with Kami. Together they watched the poor colt run and buck and kick.

"Now do you see?" Kami gasped.

Still without thinking, she climbed the fence and jumped down into the pen. Macy followed

her. They dodged Storm Cloud's hooves as he thundered past.

"Wes, stop!" Macy pleaded. "Please stop!"

She tried to grab hold of the whip, but he pushed her away.

"Back off," he snarled. "I know what I'm doing. It's called sacking out. This is how they broke colts in the old days. It teaches them to know who's boss."

"Don't!" Kami begged. "Storm Cloud is scared to death. It's cruel."

The colt twisted and turned, but still the plastic sack flapped. He neighed and reared, breaking a fence rail as he came down.

"Get out of here before I make you!" Wes ordered Macy and Kami.

Kami refused to be scared of him. "No way!" she yelled.

"This colt is crazy," Wes shouted.

"No, he's not," Kami retorted. "It's you. What you're doing is driving him crazy." She heard another horse whinny from the feed stalls and the clatter of hooves against wooden boards.

"Someone's going to get hurt," Macy warned.

As she spoke, Lady Alice appeared. She'd broken free from the stall. Kami watched as the mare saw her colt with a sack tied to his tail and Wes with a whip in his hand.

"Lady Alice – no!" Kami cried as the mare prepared to launch herself over the broken fence into the round pen.

It was no good – nothing would stop her.

Lady Alice jumped the fence then charged at Wes. He dropped the whip and backed off, raising his arms to shield himself.

Storm Cloud stopped running. His chest heaved. He trembled and sank down onto his knees.

Lady Alice reared up. She pinned Wes against the fence while Kami and Macy ran to Storm Cloud and untied the sack. Kami stroked his head and whispered to him. "Easy, boy. You're OK. Easy now. We won't hurt you."

At last Storm Cloud stopped trembling. He got back onto his feet and let Kami lead him over to the gate.

But Wes was still trapped. He was down on the ground with nowhere to go. Lady Alice reared up again. Her hooves just missed his head as she came down hard.

Then the gate opened and Jeff came in. Kami realised that he must have heard everything from the front porch and wheeled himself here.

"Dad, do something," Macy begged.

Jeff took in the scene then made his way across the round pen. Lady Alice saw him out of the corner of her eyes. She turned to him. Her ears were flat and her nostrils flared.

Would she attack Jeff or would she back away?

Slowly, slowly, Jeff pulled himself out of his chair. He showed no fear as he stood up and reached a hand out to Lady Alice.

"It's OK," he told her in a soft, calm voice. "I'm here. Everything is going to be just fine."

Chapter 6
The Truth

At last, Lady Alice was safely back in the feed stall with Candy and Pepper. Storm Cloud was next to her, eating grain from the manger.

Everyone was gathered on the front porch. Ella made Macy and Kami sit on the porch swing while Wes paced up and down.

"You don't know the full story," Jeff told them. "I need to tell you exactly what happened when I had my fall."

"We already know," Wes snapped.

"Shush and listen to your father," Ella told him. "It's important."

"No, you don't know everything."

For the second time that day Jeff stood up from his wheelchair. He took two shaky steps, put a hand on his son's arm and looked him in the eye.

"The real reason I fell off that colt was because I hadn't checked the girth strap," he said. "It was way too loose. The saddle slipped when I put my foot in the stirrup. It spooked him. I lost my balance and that's how come I fell."

"No way!" Wes stared back at him. "It was *your* fault?"

"Yes, son. Storm Cloud was no worse than any other colt getting used to having a rider on his back. It was me. I didn't want to admit it, but I was stupid."

As the news sank in, Macy opened her eyes wide and let her jaw drop. Kami took a deep breath.

"In other words, I have to re-think my training method and throw away the whip?" Wes asked.

"And the plastic sack," Jeff told him. "We don't use those methods to train colts any more. All they did was break a horse's spirit and that's not what we're aiming for."

"OK." Wes hung his head. "I get it."

'At last!' Kami thought. 'He gets it.' *Throw away the whip. Be patient, be gentle. Listen to your horse.* She turned to Macy and smiled.

"And, son," Jeff went on. "Remember, you don't have to do it all. I may not be able to ride right now, but I can listen and watch. I can give advice."

Wes looked up and nodded.

Macy sprang up and hugged her dad. "And you remember, too – you're standing and walking! You're really getting better."

"I am," he agreed. "Before you know it, I'll be back in the saddle and when I do I'll make sure the girth strap is buckled good and tight!"

Kami picked her time to make her exit. She left the family talking and walked to the feed stalls. First she untied Candy and Pepper and led them out to the meadow. Then she went back for Lady Alice and Storm Cloud.

"This is a great end to the day," she said as she walked with them in the evening sun. "Sure, there was that bit in the middle that wasn't too good."

Lady Alice walked calmly beside her while Storm Cloud gave a little crow-hop and a gentle whinny.

"But it'll all work out," Kami promised the horses, as much as herself. She knew it would take a while for Storm Cloud to forget the fear and pain of the round pen, but in the end he would.

She opened the gate to the meadow and took off the horses' halters. Lady Alice pushed Kami's hand with her nose. Storm Cloud gave another little hop then a buck.

"OK, go!" Kami said.

Storm Cloud took off. He galloped over the grass then stopped at the stream to drink. His dark coat gleamed in the setting sun.

Just beautiful.

"Go," Kami whispered to Lady Alice, who was still by her side.

The mare nuzzled her hand one last time. Then she raised her head and looked across the meadow. The water in the stream glittered gold. The grass was a rich, lush green. She set off at a slow canter, then gathered speed to gallop over to join Storm Cloud.

"I'll see you tomorrow," Kami called, with a huge smile on her face. "Yip, cow, yip! I can't wait!"

It was supper time. Kami turned to stroll back to the ranch house to join her best-friend-forever, Macy Lucas, and her family.

More from our stable of brilliant horse stories ...

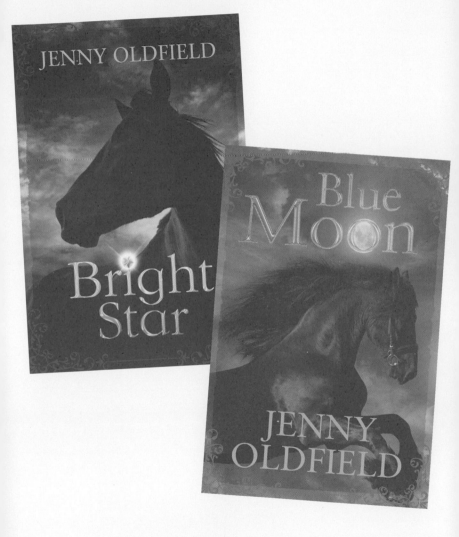